Squash the Spider!

For Chris, Ian, Mark,
Richard and Roger.
Great with computers,
useless with spiders!

SQUASH THE SPIDER!
A PICTURE CORGI BOOK 0 552 54797 2

First published in Great Britain by David Fickling Books,
an imprint of Random House Children's Books

David Fickling Books edition published 2003
Picture Corgi edition published 2004

1 3 5 7 9 10 8 6 4 2

Set in Esprit Book

Picture Corgi Books are published by Random House Children's Books,
61–63 Uxbridge Road, London W5 5SA,
a division of The Random House Group Ltd,
in Australia by Random House Australia (Pty) Ltd,
20 Alfred Street, Milsons Point, Sydney, NSW 2061, Australia,
in New Zealand by Random House New Zealand Ltd,
18 Poland Road, Glenfield, Auckland 10, New Zealand,
and in South Africa by Random House (Pty) Ltd,
Endulini, 5A Jubilee Road, Parktown 2193, South Africa

THE RANDOM HOUSE GROUP Limited Reg. No. 954009
www.**kidsatrandomhouse**.co.uk

A CIP catalogue record for this book is available from the British Library.

Printed in China

Squash the Spider!

Nick Ward

Picture Corgi

High up on the ceiling Squash
the Spider was waiting to pounce!
Billy came in to watch T.V. and
eat his supper.

He settled in front of the telly.

Billy was just about to
take a great big bite out of
his sandwich when . . .

After supper it was Billy's bedtime. "Goodnight Mum," he called. Billy snuggled under his covers and was soon fast asleep.
In a secret hiding place, Squash was already snoring, dreaming up his next trick.

At school the next day, Billy and his friends sat down on the story mat. "Ssh! Let's start with a nice quiet story," whispered the teacher, opening her book. "All about . . ."

A very noisy spider!

"Eek!" squealed the teacher.
"SQUASH the SPIDER!"

Once upon a time in a land far, far away, lived a princess. But the princess was sad because ... locked her up in a tall tower. In a corner of the room, a spider sat spinning her web.

Squash jumped!
"Yuk!" cried the whole class.
"Where's he gone?"
But Squash had completely
disappeared!

At lunchtime, Billy was in the
playground with his friends.
"I'm not really scared of spiders,"
he explained. "I was only pretending."

"Me too," said Jo.
"Who wants a crisp?"
"What flavour?" asked Billy reaching into the bag.

Jo grabbed Squash. "I'm not scared,"
she said. "Look . . ."
Jo opened her fingers. Squash wriggled
his long spidery legs and . . .

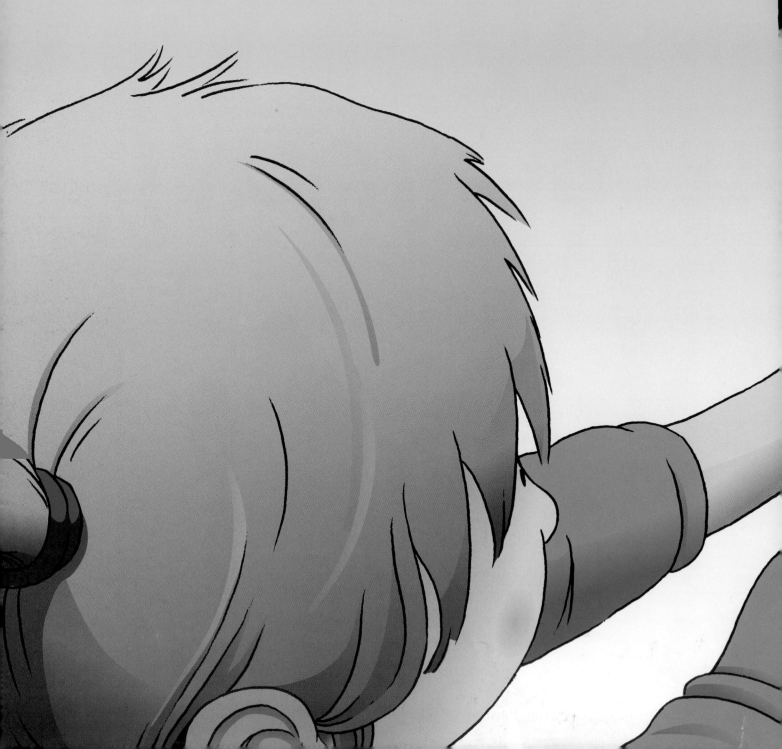

Whizz! He shot straight up Jo's sleeve.

Jo wriggled and squiggled and flapped . . .

. . . And Squash flew out of Jo's other sleeve and tumbled to the ground.

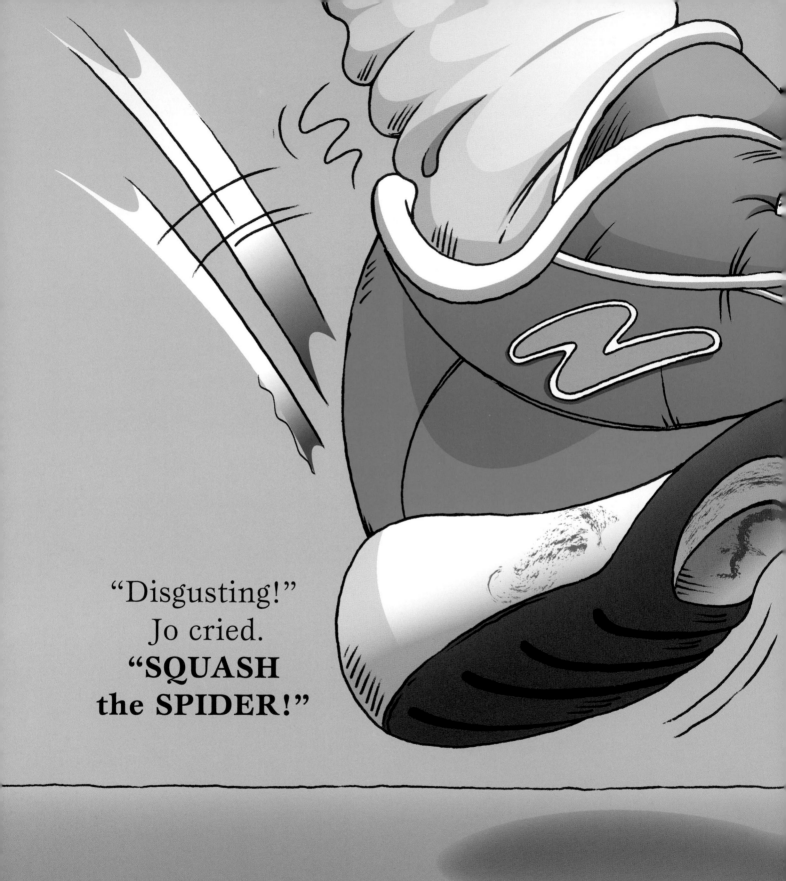

"Disgusting!"
Jo cried.
**"SQUASH
the SPIDER!"**

STO

"Phew! That was close!" gasped Squash on the way home. "But I've learnt my lesson. I will never ever ever scare anyone again!"

"Promise?" asked Billy.

"Promise!" said Squash.

And from that day on, Squash the spider never shouted "Boo!" and never ever scared anyone again.

SPIDER LANE

Well, almost never.